T0380463

Djehuty Feather

C.G. Gracey

AuthorHouse™ UK
1663 Liberty Drive
Bloomington, IN 47403 USA
www.authorhouse.co.uk
Phone: 0800.197.4150

Because of the dynamic nature of the Internet, any web addresses or links contained in this book may have changed
since publication and may no longer be valid. The views expressed in this work are solely those of the author and
do not necessarily reflect the views of the publisher, and the publisher hereby disclaims any responsibility for them.

Any people depicted in stock imagery provided by Getty Images are models,
and such images are being used for illustrative purposes only.
Certain stock imagery © Getty Images.

This book is printed on acid-free paper.

ISBN: 978-1-7283-9556-2 (sc)
ISBN: 978-1-7283-9555-5 (e)

Print information available on the last page.

Published by AuthorHouse 01/10/2020

authorHOUSE

to Spirit &
fellow feather bearers

the weight will lighten

I. Grand Motherland

A mi tofuo

Eye was in China when Luo Jia was getting to know Wang Zijun. We went fishing at a pond in the countryside, catching large fish where puffy white geese quacked and a friend of our family picked a round, yellow pear from their tree for me when I was around six. She fetched it with a metal loop attached to a long rod and it was the sweetest fruit I'd ever tasted. It was as fascinating to my child eyes, as the stone eggs laying in water pails that our aunt would leave for us to play with. Fast forward to adulthood - our aunt - Li Ming's hair was greying, and so too was grandmother Puopuo's, who seemed more frail than before. I was afraid that if Puopuo fell down, she might break. Unlike other summers in Taizhou, my pretentious American self felt a little sorry for the humility of their lives at times – after waking up, she hobbled about their 3 bedroom apartment lighting incense and praying to her ceramic Guan Yin, eat her morning medicine, read the newspaper, help out with the cooking and dishwashing, hanging up laundry to dry.

Han Nana, our Puopuo (grandma) prayed in three places : the Buddha next to a large peach seashell, seated peacefully on the wooden shelves above a vase of flowers and fruit by the kitchen and veiled beneath a red fabric looking down at us. *A mi tofu, a mi to fu..* part of a booklet of mantras to be continued at her desk, or facing the river westward from their overhanging tiled green house veranda, where Luo Yi Chun, Xiao Jia's dad, used to grow his plants and smoke.

The Book of Coming Forth by Day, written several centuries ago on papyrus scrolls finely crafted from river bed reeds, states that Spirit is ineffable and cannot be measured by time nor conceived of by our thoughts. **Atum** means « the beginning », « the source, » as well as « the end, » while *Ra* means light. **Atum-Ra,** the name given to Spirit, therefore meant the beginning and end of light.

The other name for Spirit creator was **Emen-Ra,** meaning hidden light.

Finally, God was known as **Eaau,** where « eu » meant « polarization, » and « au » meant expansion : so Eaau meant power that was polarized and expanding, creating the Universe.

More Beautiful than the Nationalists' darling, Soong May-Lin

In the land of Muoli hua – home of the nation's beloved folk song, « Jasmine Flowers"

Everytime we visit, she complains about Mao Zhedong said Dad to Nana. Nana looked up from his book – BUCHARIN & the BOLSHEVIK REVOLUTION, either from UCLA or Stanford library most likely. « She hates Mao, » says Vivian.

"Doesn't my Mom look like Soong May-Lin ? » says Puopuo (grandma). She shows us four black and white pictures of Soong May-Lin from the newspaper, held between her long elegant fingers. We had jut visited Soong's home in the cultural capital of the eastern Jiangsu province, Nanjing, a focal point for the Nationalists, Communists, and imperialists whose invasion the former united for in order to oust. Nanjing was the esteemed university city where our cousin graduated from.

"No, » Ma says.

"Yes, » says Puopuo.

"No."

"Yes."

"No."

"*Mei*. Beautiful, » like my Mom says Puopuo. « Beautiful and important, » says Jiujiu, our uncle – Mom's brother. He sits next to Dad and I on the wooden couch in the living room of their third floor apartment by the Yangtze River tributary river that surrounds the city. « Nah, » retorts Dad. « History says she's important but she was nothing special except someone who happened to be associated with politics."

"She looks like my mother, » says Puopuo again, bending towards my mother from behind the glass spectacles sitting on the tip of her nose, pointing between the glass frame and paper clippings. « Your mother was more beautiful. Mei-Lin looks like a typical Guangzhou person, short and ugly as can be, » says Dad. Vivian and I chuckle. She translates the Chinese conversation into English for Nana.

"Have some peanuts, » says Jiujiu to me.

"That's alright, we just ate dinner, » I said, belly full of rice, onion chives, chicken soup brewed with goji berries and ginger, freshwater shrimp and crabs cooked with vinegar and soy sauce, and fish. There was truly no meal in my mind worldwide other than those which my aunt cooks.

"Have some peanuts."

"I'm full though."

"You can still eat peanuts when you're full, » he says scrunching up his lips and pointing to the boiled nuts with his mouth. Similarly to the chicken eggs, they are smaller than those in the u.s., but tastier.

Puopuo says, « Look at your grandmother. Your grandfather had a great life but it became miserable because of Mao, » she points to the black and white portraits of her parents which remain from the end of dynasty and dawn of republic, amongst the only images I've seen of my great-grandparents. They are middle-aged, dressed in padded traditional peacoats and rather hardy-looking without smiles. The Communist Party, which Puo puo's father was active in, a popular mayor of the city, took over China in the 1940's shortly after uniting with the Taiwanese Nationalists who had initially united the first modern Republic of China.

"When people age and don't have a lot of contact with reality, they start ot think about old times, » says Dad. Puopuo hobbles by slowly in her slippers that pad on the hard wood floor, across the living room towards her ginseng-soaked tea jar by the foyer. She doesn't hear most of what we say.

"Why did she cut out so many pictures of Soong May-Lin ? is what I want to know, « says vivian. Someone had handed the newspaper cuttings to her and Vivian peered at them through her glasses up at us.

Di yi ge Baba Mama. Number one, Mom and Dad. Parents are the most important.

Di er, zu ni da sha ka. Xiali bu tso, Ren zhang. Ni kan, Weiwei zhangde bu tsuo. Vivian has grown up to be gorgeous.

Han Nan Taitai, our old lady *wai puo, Puopuo* wears a silk scarf folded up into a narrow strip like a tie, tied around her neck under layers and layers of clothing beneath an elegant navy peacoat. She frowns and points her finger at me.

Kwadwo Nana underlines sentences of the Marxist literature with a blue-inked fountain pen. Vivian sits next to him in the homey bamboo chair, knitting her scarf. A string of light blue thread dips between her two hands on her lap, her fingers long and elegant like Puopuo and Mom's. Her creation continues to the mother of pearl coffee table where the bundle of thread sits atop a stack of newspapers, next to peaches and oranges.

Dad reaches towards the sack of peanuts and talks loudly, with Ma, Jiujiu and Puopuo. Vivian translates for Nana and Jiujiu laughs, a fan of wrinkles around his eyes sparkling.

My grandma hates the Communists because she was part of the established aristocracy, » clarifies Vivian.

"*Gong chang ren huai.* The Maoist Communists were evil. I DARE say it ! You don't even dare to say it. The current day Communists are more corrupt than Mao Zhedong's, » says Dad.

"*Jiang Zheming geng hui* !, » exclaims Ma, about the then head of state during my final college years, who put the otherwise obscure Yangtzhe river delta tributary-surrounded city of Taizhou, in Jiangsu province 4 hours drive away from Shanghai, on the conscience map of the general populace. They attended the same high school before my parents joined a generation of 1980's brainwave immigrants, earning their PhD's in North America after attending Chongqing University of Science and Technology.

"During Mao's time, there was no such thing as corruption on the scale of today, » says Li Ming, «beautiful person. » Her bright laughter lights up the room and my ears each summer since I can remember. She walks into the living room from the kitchen and utters this to Puo puo. Everyone but Puopuo laughs.

"She told her the exact opposite of what she wants to hear, » explains Dad.

Realm of Dwat (the Netherworlds),
after Judgement in the Hall of Justice

The deceased utters, « I am associated with the almighty One in the water of Nu, » which takes the deceased back to the beginning of time. They even say that they have become one with the Creator. There was a time at the beginning when none existed except for the light of God, who created Himself. Then, the water of N U was created by the Power of Sound, from which the 9 laws of natural existence (Paut) came forth. God manifests Himself into our earthly existence through SUNLIGHT, which gives life to everything.

Dwat, the West, is the place of the light and realm of the Soul. Auser is King of that realm and all souls must do battle with the illusion of living in it.

The deceased passes through the realm of light in the constellation of Orion, which is the house of Ausar (root for the word, author, authority). In this new, purified condition, he then identifies himself as the 'keeper of the book of things that are and things that will be.'

The deceased declares that God, who is the truth, manifests Himself through reincarnation : in other words, He manifests himself through his creations.He also mentions that Est (Isis) and Nebt-Het (Nepthys), residing in the constellation of Sirius (SEPDU), who cause reincarnation to take place, adding that they 'exist in all limits as the protectresses of incarnations.' It is for this reason that we find EST and NEBT-HET standing behind AUSAR in the illustrations of plate 5.

They are described as the 2 hidden eyes of God, in the realm of the soul.

the Book of Coming Forth by Day

Birds in the marshland

Our Mom is amongst the only of her town to make it to the land of ice cream.

If you are good to me, I'll cook you food

If you are good to me, I'll grow you nice organic garlic onion chives

If you're good to me, I'll make your bed

If you're good to me, I'll be a good wife

In Jiangsu, China, the nature of the wetland seems to cleanse ones mind. It was completely quiet outside the city where we were spending the weekend by a tree nursery, save for the chirping of birds. The sky was blue, and the water calm and clear. It rippled ever so slightly with the current of the soft breeze beneath a sunny sky, the kicking of a flock of small ducks floating across the water in the distance. The air was clean. The bamboo grass and reeds grew incredibly tall, 10-20 feet. Their fluffy tufts danced in the wind.

Their voices ; the singing rowers, sounded like still rivers and black mud that are used to manufacture bricks, the same bricks that Ma made in as a teenager in a factory during Mao's communist revolution that then built the country. Their voices sounded like willow branches and bamboo reeds and grey green freshwater river crabs, as well as concrete and plastic and change.

My parents and Dada broke out into laughter upon their final song towards the end of our boat ride through the marsh. When the wooden boats we sat afloat in reached the water's edge again we split into two roofed wooden boats, the length of a car and just wide enough for two rows of people to sit facing each other. Older, middle-aged women with wrinkled faces and hands and turquoise head scarves wrapped around their faces rowed the boats forward through tranquil canals, past more groves of reeds and grasses, past small water birds with red beaks and fuzzy wings, to the interior of the park. The woman on our boat stood towards the back, stepping forward and back to move the long wooden oar through the water to propel it forward. « The rowers make around 850 Yuan a month, » Vivian said. They like their job and said they enjoy it better than farming, which they did before the park was created largely for visitors and tourist reasons. The sounds of the women's voices and the setting were rather wonderful. Dada kept singing and humming as we stepped off the rocking wood onto the still dirt at the shore. We had just sung and hummed a song together that ended with laughter seeing as no one could quite remember the words.

That was the best part of the day, my then boyfriend Elijah said later as we were at home. « I wonder if they make a similar or greater wage than before, with farming, » said Vivian.

Luo Jia proposes that Yang Yang, her son, and husband, come to *Mei guo* (beautiful country – the U.S.) first, then her family afterwards. Ma tells Luo Jia to let Xin Ming, our uncle, take care of what has been the oldest daughter Lin Ming's responsibility – grandma Puopuo.

Bu xing ! That won't work, says Li Ming, shaking her head back and forth. The other is cupping her cheeks. Her head is bobbing ever so slightly back and forth, her lips trembling, and one of her eyes twitching at the edges as if the invisible guests of wind are blowing in front of one eye. It's the same twitch that I noticed in Nai Nai's eye in the wrinkles of her sallow skin. It's also the same twitch that Wang Zijun's mother has. « I don't like her twitch, » I remember Li Ming whispering into my ear and clutching my elbow several years ago, in that close way that her and Yang Yang do.

II. Emen Ra

Dimmed Eclipse

I hold Basil in my arms as the neon colored aesthetics and holographics of the Black Panther film flash through my mind. We sat at the two front seats of the theatre, in front of J but behind Z and his blonde sidekick. They both asked me for something ; I handed Z a cup of water that stoic Basil had put in his armrest. He didn't mind our legs touching.

Before all this, Z had made it a little better.

"You remind me of my sister. Damn Connie, you're sexy, » Z said. We talked. He liked when I touched his head, scratching his scalp. He told me to be careful of the man who drove his friends' car. They burn the candles I leave and use the coconut oil, hold the roses in their teeth in Snapchat stories before the maroon petals scatter all over his carpet that he cleaned up before hearing I was visiting. Otherwise the place was something of a mess. Z is diagnosed with cancer and returns to the UAE « after being held at knifepoint by the Russians, » : J says. « His Mom had to come here and get him, » he said, telling me to stop visiting him. When I ask him why he goes there, he doesn't answer.

The morning that Z's mom comes back to bring him back to Dubai, where he goes to work in oil and gas with his father, none of his belongings are packed. Oompie is there, splashing water on his face to wake him up. After Z « beat him up, » somewhere in Lafayette.

When Oompie and I meet again in the spring, he is initially shy to recognize me, but then blurts, » I was wondering who that was. Yo, you're like my sister ; I will beat that dude up if he touches you. » I wore an olive green bathing suit which him, Wavy and Todd were staring at.

As I turned up to the parking lot, from the creek where a David Beckham doppelganger was following me, from behind a few cars was none other than the humorous, warm guy at Z's who had listened to the dread headed Japanese hapa mountain woman lecturing him – before returning home with the dazed Mexicano amigo Israel.

"Will I end up in prison if I keep on hanging out with you ? » I ask, gazing into the emerald abyss of his eyes, catching the rays of sunlight that fall into the river canyon.

"No, you're safe within a 60 foot radius of my proximity. But also no – I'm going to state jail in 30 days, July 29th. I've been to jail a few times ; prison is federal. Never prison. » I tell him how pretty his eyes are later.

Just don't lie to me, » Oompie says. He gathers up my hair and puts his hands over my neck. Then he tells me he could charge me xyz for more time with his eyes, and that we were all brothers and sisters long ago in Egypt, before hanging out with his druid hobbit friends.

Oompie McCleod speaks almost nonstop. « They call her the town bicycle, » he says of the Japanese woman who looks like a Native American. She waved around her index finger at Oompie's coked out eyes, which followed it like a dog. This was before later punching him. Her dad was the owner of the town's most well known Sushi restaurant. They sat on couches on opposite sides of the room, a Nordic pal cloaked in winter clothes between them before putting his arm around the girl. « That was the first time we'd seen each other in years, » he said. Maybe months. I can't remember ; we were both drunk. My presence and « Anyeong haseo, » brought a smile from the Korean lady, who he said could usually tell if he was drunk or not. « Like if I walk in at 3am in the morning one day she may not want to sell me something."

"I see. Well saying that to her could make her happier. » I buckled my seatbelt and we decided to hang out with his friend Drew's place by Tantra park instead of bar hopping.

"So the Japanese lady. She lives out in some open space across the street from her big brother, my friend - I need to talk to him about something. They can look at each other from each other's kitchens."

The Story of a Hero (Heru)

Once upon a time in ancient Egypt, Ausar, the eldest of five human principles, became the first king of Egypt, embracing the virtue and conviction of GOODNESS. He ruled for 28 years, 25 of which were spent outside of Kemet, speaking to humanity about justice, faith, and virtue. He did not bring an army, but rather, was accompanied by priests, musicians, and singers on his travels. **Ausar trusted in the power of HARMONY, in the conviction that we are here to develop good rather than fight evil.** He taught the art of agriculture, encouraging the cultivation of fruit and vegetables (in preference to cannibalism).

Ausar, his name meaning vision of authority, was born on July 15th, the first of 5 intercalary days. The creation of the five human principles was a cosmic event, observed by the immortals of Etelenty and the beings of light, who stood in the GOLDEN LIGHT of the rising Sun, dressed in fine white linen, and sang a morning song, which awakened even the dead. Baboons raised their hands to the heavens, scorpions stood still, chicks burst out of their eggs, cattle became pregnant, fish leapt with joy in the water of the Nile River, and fig trees grew heavy with fruit, palm trees with dates, and vines with dark purple grapes.

Barley and wheat sprang up and the Nile flooded with green water from the far south, rendering Egypt's land fertile. Ausar was given authority over the water of the Nile and its banks, which facilitate life for all.

Beautiful Asian goddess

The dark night of the soul didn't last forever. It never does. Because light overcomes darkness. It does. Saturn passes the place it was when you emerged from the womb after 27 years – the wheel turns.

There's a public health epidemic in Colorado when I return from overseas. As I drive the blue minivan home up the Shanahan Ridge facing the blue Rocky Mountains, a wriggly sensation in my stomach –a butterfly – passed through as I listened to the replaying hits of 98.5 KYGO country radio : « When I Drink Tequila » and « If It's Meant to Be, It'll Be."

To myself : a love song :

Before Valentines Day in February, J keeps visiting his mother who is hospitalized in the ICU, and is sad about his aunt's death. A black girl in their community, a Caribbean CU student crashes her car and passes away in the accident. I kneel by him, hug him, wonder why I am not invited in to help uplift their circle, not knowing that each visit to the pullout mattress in the basement of Z's house was a waste of my time. He is strung out on Xanax, coke, drugs, and alcohol and not even there any more. « Connie, » Z says from the other room, at the same time as J asks me whether I want to get closer to him. I had been visiting Z every few days to give him a plant and red tigers' eye. To hold him. He negotiates with visitors from other parts of Colorado, maintains communications with Mexicans in Texas who he goes to visit, where he was born, and repetitively plays « Notice Me » by Cardi B's hubby Migos. Rather serious for college. The Puerto Rican Aaron, moves out and back to Denver after Anja has a panic attack. A young hobo tries to move in their extra room but Parker and I advise Z against allowing it.

On Friday, McCloud and Oli were at their pal's up the street from Nick and Willy's. The young man who appears as an unassuming thin man comes out of the second floor of a small rustic wood cabin.

"Yo."

"What's up."

We put our arms around each other beneath the spruce trees, and he grimaces when I hug him because Todd punched him in the ribs, with all his metal rings on. This was the same day after we all saw each other, when Todd and Wavy then proceeded to take $400 from him before I « saved » him from University and 44th St, a few blocks towards the mountains from where the Persian Indian Texan was running his trap house.

While J said that Z was the biggest dealer in the city, he certainly was not the most locally knowledgeable, and also didn't last long, given the story Oompie McCloud confirmed of his being flown back to Dubai by his Mom. « We know this town anyways, » he says.

He was drunk on a bottle of caramel patron, as usual sitting in the passenger's side of his biffle's ride. Not trying to holler at nobody though : I supposed soju, purchased from a middle aged Korean woman at a store next to the Dark Horse saloon we had entered and left, the night of June 21, after the doorman called out his name. He wasn't there. The « poor heartbroken Irish boy » looks at me, in his black shirt and silver chain. He keeps remarking how soft my skin was. We didn't go in the bar because he was banned. « Hey let's go hurry to the old Asian woman ; we have 5 minutes before her store closes, » he remarks about the 11 :55 time in the blue minivan. I drove through the parking lot, past McDonald's to the liquor store, and followed the skinny boyish young man into the store on the first night of that summer.

Loving yourself. Is a fulltime job. Don't give it to anyone else. But God (What I didn't know then).

"I'm with this beautiful Asian Goddess."

"Officer Shneble here."

"Team red, Team Red...yes, we're gonna need some backup here. The Russians are coming, the Russians are coming."

He admires my features. « What the FUCK !? » « OH MY GODDDDDdd. You are a pimp !"

"You're beautiful. » he says winking. « How did you know, I like smart sexy Asian women ? You are sooooo sexy. You just sexed me into submission."

Whether or not these are the same Russians who allegedly held Zahrir at knifepoint before the langy college sophomore snitched – Oompie theorizes – as a means of evading persecution due to the clout of his wealthy family, I wouldn't doubt. This was Colorado. How many Russian mobsters could there be?

McCloud keeps saying we have « chemistry, » talking about how Wavy and Todd robbed him before I saved him, where someone pulled a pistol from their underwear (using a slang word I didn't recognize), how him and Drew, a more relaxed version of Z's roomie Spencer kept bugging him throughout the night, and also that they knew and worked with Mohamed, Jj's younger brother for a few years now. Neither him nor Drew slept much that night.

Oompie kept blabbing as we sat on Robbie's living room couch. We drove to the PDQ on Baseline, the gas station, where he insisted I go inside to watch him commit fraud – or at least force an old 60-year-old man who he knew personally to commit fraud – by using a noncredit card, with a punched hole in it and a portrait of himself with long hair. Every few minutes we're talking, he « Zzzzz's » or « HONNNNN's, » pretending to fall asleep.

"Yo you're dope as fuck. Yo, I got your back, » his expression is stoic and his eyes gleam with mischief.

Back in the navy van, he asks if I take birth control, then insists that I take plan B within three days instead of a test, which he says you have to wait a week for (turns out to be inaccurate ; it can be taken immediately). « I'm not taking any chances, » he fusses. « Not after seeing an unborn fetus with my hair covered in blood die on a linoleum floor. » His ginger stubble, black head hair. « I peaked when I was 14. My life is like going back to 2nd grade after getting a PhD."

"I'm going to roofie Plan B into you."

"No you're not. And also, as I already stated, I'm not taking it."

He chuckles. I'm funny.

I park the van in front of Nick's house, bracing myself for more adventure.

"The bloods, Crips, Southside, north side, east, west, Southwest, Latin bloods, Aryan brotherhood, MS-13, Asian Triads – they're ALL here babes. Colorado is exactly in the middle of it ; all the forces are present. I know them all, and they all want to kill me."

« Don't mix any of your belongings with mine. Just do what I say. Don't lie to me, » he pinches my arm.

"Ok. Did you see Black Panther ? Maona, Lady Bird, Star Wars ?"

"I didn't see any of those, I've been under a rock. I'm just a poor heartbroken Irish boy. »

Oompy blabs about our meeting to the big cool black guy Todd next time he saw him, probably to procure analogue. Todd the 39 year old hits him in the abdomen.

I see Jj. Jj goes to Chicago, Illinois to visit his younger brothers who moved there. Sudani African brothers living the d r e a m, he says, from underneath his K'naan Abdi Warsame-style fedora hat.

Afro Todd and his Filipino friend J and I hang out with Ollie at our spot at the bend of the creek on the south bank – Ollie is with Courtney one time, then not another. Todd tells me what Oompie said ; that he had been seeing me.

Why yes – he had been seeing me.

The clouds are poofy, against a blue sky.

They stick out like limbless and headless sheep, and at sunset are colored a pleasant light, warm, peachy range of orange throughout. The texture of the brown flatirons pop and mountain terrain deepens, the sun shines a little more relentlessly.

Over time, the physique of J changes. From unsightly, to fitting. This seems to happen, magically, with Todd and New York David as well ; the size of their bodies shrink and become more manageable. People do say that Boulder is magic. Love and lust, however, are not the same. Truth can bend illusion only for so long. « Be nice to yourself, » Todd says on the phone. After weeks of being grumpy to me.

Kiss full of color makes me wonder where you've always been

I was hiding in doubt when you brought me out of my chrysalis

I Came out new

Your life will lead you to dark places, when you fail to face the light within. If you don't already know, it's brighter than you may be capable of comprehending. That's all we are : love-light. My family tried to show me the way with their lanterns. It's as if, somehow, I didn't know.

I feel so in the present moment, as Todd and I chat about how Oompie stole, though we love him and he helped Todd in a time of need. « Steal tha car, » Oompie text me. « Hahaha."

Todd admits to punching him in the Dark Horse. That's why they both have their pictures hanging on the bulletin board inside the bar and are banned from entry. « That's the homie, » Miya says of him.

At the gas station on Arapahoe next ot the vacated Wendy's we used to go to when we were little, I am full of love towards this beautiful Asian goddess woman in the mirror. « I'm fine, » I say to Oompie, who calls back the next day asking how I am.

"I know you are."

I'm attracted to Todd, and we smoke a bowl over the night view of Viele Lake, our words touching each other like honey. « I can support you from time to time. » Our hands touch and I face away towards the lake in the dark valley below, framed by the curve of the mountain range. He's closer the ridge, which is at a slight incline up from the water system. He grabs my neck and touches me.

Wavy chuckles when I change hammocks to Ollie's hammocks. Ollie chuckles when I move back to Ollie's. It's a sunny day and the light is shining through the leaves. It is hanging a bit higher up than the other, and also because Ollie is younger, only 23, I don't want to squish him despite his strong build. He doesn't have fingerprints on his hands. We relax and enjoy the breeze blowing through the tree branches above us, the flow of the creek.

Todd is not at all amused, and lays in his hammock grumpily behind his dark sunglasses. I walk over to his hammock next to the water slowly. He spreads his legs and tells me to go away. « Trouble, » he mumbles. That's what Oompy said when he met me as well : trouble.

Me I never care what the badman say.

he Democrats say that people and nonprofits are people, not big pharm. At what point do ADDICTS become responsible for themselves ? When I left Colorado, I never even referred people to recovery programs or rehab. The shoes hang from the telephone lines by their laces. And my generation wastes itself, choosing addiction over humanity, reverting to old habit in the face of what Bernie Sanders has called for : a revolution. Even a reLOVEution won't change a tweaker though. Only a tweaker can change a tweaker. With a lightness in my heart, I left. We're not young kids anymore;; millennials.

As I drove the boys back to Z's from the town cinema after the movie, past pine trees, a moon gleams like an eye in the sky, staring at us. I dropped them off ; we were all quiet after hearing SZA and Lamar's songs – this time not on the summer radio, but amidst the chill of early winter. After I went home, I couldn't fall asleep in my silky bed. I longed to be held, acknowledged. To be in an artistic creative environment. I bid the curfew that Dad set.

Power girl, I really wanna know your ways.

I want the credit if I'm winning or losing, that's the realest.

I did not go to Basil's as J texted. At some point, a panther scratched the aspen in the front yard like it did to our neighbors some decade and a half ago : deep scars that say, « I was here. » Even that this is theirs. Images of rabbits beheading snakes and people thrashing swords at each other flashed through my head and prevented me from sleeping, even beneath the comfort of the down comforter in my sister's warm room; anywhere closer to her protection. An intense shattering pain exploded inside my chest, as if my heart was breaking into a million pieces.

The person who had brought me to this point: down the street with kids half a decade younger than us. He wasn't in New York or Africa or another one of the many countries he had said, let's go fly away to visit – he was down the street a 10 minute drive away.

The Story of a Hero (Heru), a Hawk : Thank You Jesus

Ausar (Osiris') absence from Egypt gave his brother, Set (Satan) 25 years to hatch a plot against him with the help of 72 conspirators including the Queen of Ethiopia Aso. Set constructed a chest of cedar wood in the shape of a man with Oser's exact measurements (5 m 14 cm), inlaid with golden leaves and a thousand gems of carnelian and turquoise. On its lid, Oser's face was depicted in black, shining ebony with lips of carnelian and eyes of bright lapiz lazuli and ivory. On the side of the chest was a portrait of NUT (HEAVEN), with a deep blue body and a belly spangled with yellow stars. Queen Aso of Ethiopia aid her charms of eternity, sleep, and binding over the chest.

Upon Oser's return, Set held a banquet for him in the city of Abdu (Abydos). Oser embraced his brother and kissed him on the cheeks, glad that Set had forgotten their differences. Set brough his gift, wrapped in white linen, and offered it to whoever could lie in it and fit exactly. Everyone cheered but one by one, no one could fit into the chest exactly as it was too tall. They persuaded Oser to try his luck, and when he relented and lay down inside, the conspirators slammed the lid but on him and nailed it closed with iron nails, filling the cracks between the lid and box with melted lead. The guests who tried to save Oser could not lift the lid which was heavily inlaid with jewels and metals. The conspirators hacked at them with their swords and spears, and the rest of the guests ran away.

Set and his 72 conspirators carried the chest to the river and threw it in the Nile, saying « He drowns in his own waters. He is trapped in form, inert. He is cut down like his own stalks of wheat. Ever after, his name shall be 'Still heart, ruler of the land of the Dead.' With a cry of victory, Set ran back to the palace, where he drank Oser's drink, ate his honeyed cakes, and ordered about and beat his brother's servants. Then he fell asleep in the soft, perfumed sheets of his brothers' bed.

III. Feather of Truth

Our second day in DongYang东阳 we drove to the base of the mountain that our Lu family once owned, and connected to Spirit by burning money for Yeye's parents at their gravestones. The green, nipple-shaped mountain had belonged to the family until Chairman Mao Zhedong's CCP expropriated land from Chinese families. Mom, Dad, Vivian and I walked uphill past a school on a narrow dirt path past tall thin trees with eye-shaped leaves, with Yeye Nainai, Junhao, and Jiajia. We passed rock and fern clusters up to the left to a clearing where the vegetation thinned to grass. There rested also the memorials of other ancestors – Yeye's father's parents, and his *Gege's* (older brother) wife – three generations. Wreaths of shiny silver paper folded into pyramids were brought out of plastic grocery bags and burned in two piles. There were also dozens of red origami pyramidal forms, sewn onto a thread like beads on a bracelet thread.

They resembled the shape of traditional money and weights that were used before the modernized republic, like wonton dumplings with a slight rotund bulge in the middle. Pillars of smoke rose above the two piles of flames that Junhao let and Yeye fanned. Jijia sheaved rectangular, fake American mei yuan into the flames and handed us piles of the currency to offer to the ancestors. Mom and Dad shuffled between the two piles amongst us, adding sheaths of plain metallic papers that burnt up with the medley of flaming papers. Sticks of long incense were lit and placed in front of the graves, streams of smoke disappearing into the summer breeze.

The graves were supposedly moved since the last time our family visited four years ago. Dad told us that Junhao is opportunistic and moved the bones, according to tradition. I remember visiting Yeye's parents graves before when they had been in that original location. Still left of the rice paddies, but higher up in the terrain and imbedded in a nearly hidden place through thick overgrowth of bushes which Yeye had to search through with a stick for a few minutes.

The last time we visited Dong Yang, Vivian almost got hit by a bu son the same road that our grandfather was killed on, towards the city from the mountain as our family was casually crossing it back. We were all walking back. The cars on the road came speeding down a slight hill for several meters from the right as you leave the mountain and walk towards the city. Dad grabbed Vivian by her arm and pulled her out of the way just in time.

~

Eat, eat, eat: the highlight activity in China. We eat. Kong qing cai (empty fresh leafy spinach), duck cooked with medicinal herbs and dates, simple dough noodles with pork and bok choy, and snails for lunch at a restaurant. Junhao says he wants to open a similar restaurant.

"Are there 108 beads?" asks our uncle Bing Bing, of the wooden necklaces that he gifted us to remember Dong Yang by. That is how many prayers the Buddhists and Muslims count on their prayer strings. He goes off another travel tale, and Yeye and Nainai get their own lighter, more sandy, and turquoise colored globes between their hands, bead by bead along the string with a thumb as if counting them.

We pass an hour or two eating stir-fried crabs with soy sauce, emerald xian cai (pickled vegetables), red fermented rice pancakes with pulled pork, abalone cooked in a gelatinous yellow broth, a chicken soup cooked with mushrooms and oval dates, steamed freshwater shrimp that turn from grey to orange, and the Dong Yang signature: succulent turquoise *dong gua* winter melon cooked with pieces of ham.

Bing Bing and Nai Nai spoke in Putuong hua, so I understood bits and pieces. Bing bing turned off the dinner with what felt like an 8-minute speech, in a booming voice recounting his travels to see the world. He never received formal education, which seemed to have no bearing on his success as a businessperson. He and our grandfather, Yeye's cousin, and his mother, had operated retail shops in the country's westernmost Xinjiang province that borders Afghanistan, Tibet, Russia, and Kazakhstan. His thick dark eyebrows and beard, large eyes, and heavyset Genghis-Khan like build don't serve to persuade my sister and I of his temerity. There in Xinjiang, they learned the local languages such as Uiyger, and sold household items like blankets and shoes.

"I wanted to go to Ukraine and North Africa, but we decided to stay in Dongyang for the time being," he announces, large eyes gleaming. "It's more safe here, where I can continue to develop our business locally. There's too much social unrest in those places abroad," he says waving his hands. He captivates everyone's attention and brings forth many chuckles from the older relatives.

"Dongyang is my home, and after all, home is still the best place of all."

Nai Nai holds his broad shoulders, picks out a piece of rice from his point black beard and chuckles affectionately. "Yes, that's right. Dongyang is our home."

Bing Bing turns to his daughter, a chubby third grader who is a spitting image of him. "Go talk to the American aunties now! Say what you practiced in the car."

Bing Bing's daughter came over to us shyly as children are around strangers.

"Hello, how are you?" says Vivian.

"Heddo. I ama fine, sank you," she says. She looks at us and we look at her.

"Did you like living in Xinjiang province?" I ask. She pauses.

"No. there were...*zhenme shuo*...there." Ma translates the word I didn't understand as "terrorists."

"In Kazakhstan and Moscow, USSR I had all sorts of adventures!" our uncle tells my grandparents the next day over lunch. Nai Nai had already told us about some of them the night before as we returned to our hotel rooms. She was excited. The bed sheets and pillowcases were clean and white. Bing Bing's mother was a strong woman, Nai Nai told us, grasping our arms.

Living in Xinjiang province was not easy. The Native American-looking Dong Yang aunts and uncles, distant relatives on Dad's side of the family, were scrutinized and looked at differently than

Han people. Hans, the majority ethnic group in China, were regularly inspected by the Xinjiang law authority there and stripped of dignity despite their honest intentions as salespeople.

One day the Xinjiang law came to inspect Bing Bing's mother's home. She was fed up of being harassed by checks and searches! So she took a knife and slashed open their cardboard boxes of clothes to show the police officers that all the items they traded were in fact legal.

Atum creating the Universe via sound

"Atum-Ra felt the desire to begin the work of creation and uttered the sacred word to create. This sound brought the world to life in the form of an egg out of the water of NU. From this egg came forth the light of God.

Ra, the light of God in nature, was later manifested on earth through the disk of the sun, Aten, and appeared for the first time in the form of Dsher, or the sunrise at the beginning of life upon earth.

When light came forth upon earth for the first time, the first humans, in the form of 8 primordial humans, were created in ETLENTY (Atlantis) when water – the TEARS OF GOD, who cried for future humans – and mixed with the earth's soil."

Dong Yang, China

Before Yeye's father was killed by a car on the road in front of the family's mountain, he had been writing letters to Yeye telling him to return to Dong Yang. This was the same mountain which our relatives scoured, hunting for a tiger whose bones they bottled for medicine, which sneakily dragged away a man to death from a campfire before anyone in the circle even noticed. The same mountain that Yeye ran down without stopping as a teenager, terrified after being asked by Japanese soldiers to carry some supplies and help them build their (later to be abandoned and dismantled, after their surrender to the Allies after Pearl Harbor and axis loss during WWII) watch camp from the top of the mountain. The backdrop of a traditional, four household-shared courtroom home in front of a pond connected to rice paddy canals. Probably not far from the field where Nai Nai was born, in the dead of winter.

Dad says that great grandfather was intending to tell his middle son and most kind, tall, brave, and handsome of them, our Yeye where in the mountain he had hidden his will, but he passed away before Yeye returned home. A feud and treasure hunt amongst his three sons ensued, and remained pursued by the most adamant of descendants to this day – Junhao, the youngest descendent of the youngest son – but still no one had found the will. Coming across great grandfather Lu's loot may not have been Junhao's motive for digging up the graves. Why, then, did he move the couples graves to a spot amongst the pine forest in front of the mountain, that was less conspicuous than before?

At dinner, we went to a block of the city with old buildings belonging to the Chan clan. They were painted white with black tile roofs and black flowers, with gorgeous flowering ribbon-like plant designs painted over. Our Nai Nai's namesake, Zhang, a mainland version of the Chan migrants from Taiwan: probably the same Chan in Buddhist history. On this block were two properties owned by two of Nai Nai's step brothers, and her biological brother who resembled her quite a bit. Nai Nai's inherited property was her space in my heart. As a woman, following the patriarchal tradition, she did not inherit land. Her younger step brother owned four units of stores, about half a block – 2 shops, and a restaurant, with apartments several floors above them that we went up to.

We hung out at his apartment a little bit, with Yeye, Nai Nai, Nai Nai's didi and his wife before heading downstairs for dinner. We were sitting in a private room enjoying spicy pickled fish soup with everyone when Nai Nai's didi's son and his wife and daughter arrived. I was enjoying the salty and sour slices of white fish floating with pickled *cai* (bok choy veggies) in a chili broth, as we slowly broke into the food anticipating the arrival of Nai Nai's didi's older daughter's family.

(albino) allig8ers eat shit,

& they ain't say nothing.

100mafo's can't tell me nothing.

The sun, warming us each day, even there from behind the
other side of Earth all night, as we orbit him.

We Bee's in the center,

Bee Bee's in the center

We Bee's in the center,

Bee Bee's in the center

The moon, made from us, orbiting us

Waning and waxing, pulling and pushing the eggs in womans' ovaries out and back in like the tides of the oceans. Out and in. What did it feel like when you gave birth to me? Are we enmeshed when apart? How can I help you? When do her and the sun ever share the same sky?

Detaching detachment, in order to follow their own pathways. And yet seemingly in constant dance; following; of each other.

Sun and Moon. Earth and her shared sky. Palette for the cosmos ways. sun centricity, moon centricity, earth centricity, human centricity

Heard 'bout all kinds of centricities

How about Kindness centricity

Leaving Etlenty

The four couples which left Etlenty in nearly the same order they were created: first dark Kek & Keket, born at dusk, then Heh & Hehet, the Asiatic dawn peoples, Nun & Nunit, the mid-day Europeans, and finally Emen & Emenet the Egyptian forefathers – though created before, at sunrise along with Heh & Hehet.

Fuzhou福州

In the morning, I pushed through droopy eyes and a headache with clear, golden jasmine oolong tea in a short ceramic cup at breakfast. By the way Nai Nai was talking to Dad, Ma, Viv and us, I felt on edge. My family too was a little anxious I guessed, even if we don't show it on our faces or movements - Nai Nai's moods can be rather unpredictable.

After breakfast, Nai Nai went to our parent's room and lectured them – mostly Dad – for two hours or so. It was here in her home where her and Yeye grew up, inland from where he did in Fuzhou where they migrated to later start a family, that she was angry at Dad for not talking to her during the bi-weekly phone calls he made to their Fuzou apartment number from Tincup Circle, Colorado. She berated him.

"I care about you," said Dad. These words seemed to make Nai Nai switch gears.

"*Hao.* Good," her warm, sharp crackly cackle. "Now repeat that." Ye Ye walked into the room.

Yes or No?

Do We want them to visit?

The Annunaki lived on an iron-rich planet called Nibiru, whose lakes and rivers were red. Their perception and influence on time and time travel abilities were beyond what we can imagine. Planet Nibiru's atmosphere became clouded over time, and they sought gold in order to clear it because the metal could be used to reflect the head that was clouds and combustion. The closest source of that metal: planet Earth.

With rainbows in my being:

if you can have mercy on us -- yes.

Perhaps, when I told them that I loved them with all of my heart, it was some force you're connected to, that these words were meant for. What does the moon say to the sun, or the Earth? What say them to the Sun – how do they begin?

These words were meant for the people

who feel my sunlight; who gave it to me

~ ~

Yeye Nai Nai invited me to go to China to teach English for a few months. Their tone was loving.

The anger that I had come to expect from Nai Nai did not come, it was controlled and channeled into dismay. Her and Yeye didn't argue with Mom and Dad like they did when Vivian and I had visited Fuzhou as kids!

We left Dongyang on good terms with them in what felt like the first time in years.

However, the last night in Fuzhou, I barely slept a wink as a mosquito kept returning to BUZZZZ its shrill, high pitched piercing into my ears every few minutes, as I helplessly flapped at then applied smelly Tiger balm ointment onto the headboard of the bed.

My sister looked peaceful and unperturbed. It wasn't the mosquitoes or jet lag though; this feeling of sadness in me, after our 2 week visit. We'd adjusted to the 12 hour time difference. Nai Nai's cries echoed in my chest and gnawed at it; a thick, heavy lump of grey matter, anxiousness.

Nai Nai often reminded us of how difficult her life had been. Looking back now, maybe we didn't deserve it even if it was true. That was her truth. She is a crazy woman, a beautiful one: Zhang Nan Sheng. Maybe that's just what people need to hear. Are people today more or less willing to give their lives up for their friends than before? Her strife didn't necessarily make my parent's flight look better from where us race-conscious "model minority" and 2nd generation survivor's guilt-bearing millennials stood; their excelling as professors of the brain drain and sending of daughters to top universities.

Their happiness, my heaven, however, was theirs to claim and mine to protect.

Their dream, Their journey, risks, bravery, and Faith, the springboard from which we sprung, the air beneath our wings

Is there a word for the way that I'm feeling tonight?

Happy and sad at the same time

You got me smiling with tears in my eyes, 'cause I'm happy and sad at the same time

They say everything that goes up must come down

I don't want to come down

Those summers when we visited China were happy. Relieving, upon return, yet blue as well,

sky blue

There are few faults in the Universe.

There is a lot of emptiness; nothingness.

Rainbows and light; compassion and pure, unfiltered kindness. Acts of
kindness over and over that make the stars shine and rainbows rain and the
sun glow and moon gleam and earth fluff and turn – that's what I say.

In the morning, birds sing

Hawks fly overhead, and rain nourishes pear and apple trees whose babies
have heard my songs and words and bird songs and whose mama papa have
felt my hands around their branches and trunks and hugs. **The fruit is a Gift**.
I hold the fruit and watch it ripen; half a week in a basket in the sun

inside of me, Smiles

i am light; pure, rainbow, light

This dawn, day, and darkness is my heaven because I am 27

The LaGuardia h.s. for performing arts is @Amsterdam & Bernstein

by the geffenplayhouse & Lincoln metropolitan opera center, nyc PHILHARMONIC

Lightness of the soul: I am balanced, I am whole. In Love

Oh winged guardian angels

Thank you for protecting and freeing

Thank you for allowing me to be a vessel for your light and work, and allowing me to
profess my truth which is that I would give up anything for my loved ones, and that I
would give my life in order that your work be executed. In Heru's mama name amen.

Reincarnation & Dwat

Dwat, the West is the place of light and realm of the soul. Oser rules that realm and all souls have tot
do battle with the illusion of living in it.

The deceased's actions are weighed on the scales of justice against a feather of truth. They pass through
the constellation of Orion, the house of Oser. Est & Nebt-Het, the « two hidden eyes of God, in the
realm of the soul, » reside in the constellation of Sepdu (Sirius), and cause reincarnation and creations
to exist as the protectoresses of incarnations.

Zhang Nan Sheng : in memorandum

Ye Ye and his younger brother were born of peasant parents. They didn't attend college, unlike Nai Nai whose father was a commander in the Nationalist Party and college buddies with the Party's succeeding leader Jiang Jieshi (commemorated in American Chinatown's as Chiang Kai Shek in Cantonese). Nai Nai, Zhang Nan Sheng, attended college, collected at least four bookshelves of classical literature, and used to call Yeye "illiterate."

Yeye and his didi were recruited by the Communist Party due to personal "backdoor" connections, he says.

In the afternoon, we visited Bing Bing's home, a capacious 2 story building with huge 20-feet tall doors underneath a traditionally fashioned gateway. The adults chatted up above the tiled roof of the gate with upwards pointed corners, for a few minutes over mango juice and grapes, and then showed us the family's garden across the road in the front: fields of corn, rows of a lettuce-like vegetable, stalks of two feet long cucumbers and beans with purple blossoms climbed up the sloped terrain surrounding a pond. The old women seemed happy and proud to show us what they were growing, the garden fertilized with cow manure. In the water, a dozen ducks quacked and floated with grace over the surface, while koi fish swam about and pecked at the surface.

We went to meet up for dinner with one of Nai Nai's younger brothers. The women at the table were pretty and went about eating.

Zhang Nan Sheng started speaking louder and louder. She seemed irritated and left the room. The rest of us continued eating but after ten minutes or so, Ye Ye and Dad went to check on her. She had gone upstairs to her younger brother's apartment and was standing by the entrance in the foyer of the living room in front of the T.V. and balcony.

"How dare they not address us. I raised you since you were a baby!" she berated him, swearing. Her face was blotched with rage so Vivian and I retreated back to the other room, across the landing. As we picked at the rice with our chopsticks, and cai from the lazy susan, her shouts from across the landing and through the walls.

We lost our appetite and then left in a hurry and consoled Nai Nai that it was OK, as she hurled insults at the younger generation for their lack of showing respect and manners.

Nai Nai was about the age of those relatives, 15, an adolescent when she lost her father to his suicide. This was after he had remarried her mother's younger sister after her mother died shortly after giving birth to her. Left to take care of her aunt's sons and live with them, she allegedly had a rocky upbringing.

That night I couldn't sleep, a heavy weight in my chest as if hindering my breathing and pulse.

~

Ye Ye was stationed as a radio journalist content editor in charge of over 100 bureaucrats in Zhejiang, Shanghai, South Korea, and Fuzhou in 1952 starting when he was 22. Nai Nai came out from their hometown in Zhejiang, to the coast in Fuzhou 5 years later or so. The coast is about 60 miles away from Fuzhou, which is as far as Dad says the Nationalists, attempting to spread their domain from the island of Taiwan, ever made it.

This morning is spring: the plum blossoms are blooming, purple, and cinnamon scented, and Ye Ye walks peacefully through the park behind their home through a vermillion pavilion beneath a temple we visited before Nai Nai left us. Dad and I walk to the mountain and look around a temple at its base not far from where the Communist military station was that Ye Ye was stationed at and the apartment complex where they used to live. It's still there, red star, soldier standing in a glass box with a hand to his head.

It's been a year since Nai Nai passed.

Lania' Kea means « immense heaven » in Hawaiian, Akea meaning spacious, immeasurable as suggested by Nawa'a Napoleon, an associate professor of Hawaiin language at Kapiolani Community College – honoring Plynesian navigators who used their knowledge of the stars to navigate the Pacific. Scientists theorize that like a lung inhaling breath and tree of life growing, it is expanding.

All the stars are not closer.

People lie, the one you thought you would spend your life with. It doesn't stop me from enjoying my breath and loving my life now.

Lania'Kea is breathing : even if you didn't move, you still moving. Even if you didn't breath, you still part of a breath. Within it as we speak, we are located by a certain stream of divine energy, is our galaxy, within which lies our relatively miniscule solar system, inside of which, we observe components of – chasing each other like never-touching wings.

There's a story that Nai Nai told us multiple times over the years. Not about how she came to be called "difficult birth" and how she was born in the dead of winter in the middle of a field, because her mother did not feel safe going to the hospital during the Japanese occupation of China – as the soldiers would sometimes execute sick Chinese people to prevent disease spreading. (She was a good deal younger than our Ye Ye). Not about what we liked to do when we were little babies, before we could remember, how Dad had to cover Vivian's eyes for a few moments before she would open them or how I cried a lot. Not about how gorgeous my mother was and how much Dad loved her. The story goes, that the family was traveling from Dong Yang to Fuzhou.

By this time, the Nationalists governed the country and the Communists had not yet been conceived of as Dad was just a small child. On the table of the train compartment, there was a bowl with a peach.

Dad insisted on giving it to her even though there was only one.

The Story of a Hero (Heru)

No, I've never been this far off of the ground

They say everything that goes up must come down

The chest floated down the Nile river until it reached the city of Byblos by the Mediterranean Sea where it became encased by the growth of a tree, which was then cut and used as a pillar in the Royal Palace there. Oser's wife Est dressed up as a commoner in order to gain entrance to the palace, where, upon meeting her, the Byblos royalty granted her access to Oser's body which she brought back in one.

Coming to represent chaos in the midst of natural order, or *ma'at*, which his older brother upheld, Set made his namecase in history as Satan by hacking Oser's body into 13 pieces which he scattered Egypt. Whether or not this was motivated by the fact that his wife, Est's syster Nebt-Hebt, and her decided to play a trick on him by having Nebt-Hebt bear a jackal dog-headed son by the name of Anubis by way of Set's brother and not him, Nebt's husband, who knows. The siblings, as grandchildren of the sky goddess and earth god couldn't help their larger than life presences, and thus, larger than life rivalries.

Devastated, Est went around Kemet (the black land fertilized by the Nile's flooding) and Desherret (the red deserts), which unified represent the unification of Egypt's order and chaos into one, collecting all the pieces of her husband's corpse.

She brings Oser's body back to lower Egypt, and magically in bird form was able to breath life back to him briefly enough for them to conceive of a son, Heru, known to the Greeks and Greek translator Herodotus as Horus - who was born with the body of a human and head of a hawk. Isis hides from Set in the reeds to raise Heru.

Est walks amongst ordinary people who are unaware of her identity, and divine healing powers. With their help grieving Est was able to raise Heru and cure him of snake and scorpion bites. As heir to the throne, though just a boy, Heru was Set's political threat, and in a series of contests to determine who would succeed Oser's throne, they fought each other as hippopotami, boat raced, and even engaged in other forms of intercourse.

Tehuty the deity of the moon brought language into being, using language to foretell the future of humanity. Working with other deities, they created relics that remain to this day, when creation was still occuring. It was Tehuty who ordered the emigration of the four pairs out of Etelenty knowing of its submergence by the ocean to come - referred to in later records as the great flood. Before this, the primordial beings there witnessed the creation of the moon from the soil of the Atlantic Ocean, and other life forms.

So, the primordial of ancient knowledge was still alive when it came time for court judgement of Heru versus Set before Set's father Geb, who had sided with his son thus forth.

The story lives within all of us; an eye behind our eyes yet to be recognized. The Eyes of Horus, like the waxing and waning phases of the moon, are torn out by Set in yet another one of his merciless advances. In a final verdict, Djehuty mediates restores rulership to the one who can fly, Horus. Est and her sister lived out a happy peaceful life by the waters edge maintaining as much order as possible, greeting Creator's golden light each morning with open arms like those of an eagle's wings.

Printed in the United States
By Bookmasters